To...

One day you will discover the secret.

From...

Archie And The Secret Through The Ivy.

Written and illustrated by Adam Gibbs

Dedicated to...

GRANDMA &
GRANDAD

(Mum & Dad)

Chapters

Hi, my name is Archie. I'm 6 3/4 and I like to visit my grandaparent's and play in my grandad's garden. This is my friend Micky - he is also 6 3/4.

I have known Micky all my life. He can be quite mischievious at times, often wispering some very naughty ideas into my ear.

'Hey don't forget about me!'

Oh yeah, this is my little sister Sophie, who likes to skip a lot. She is 5 1/4 and - I like to call her 'Lil Sophie.

Read on to find out what rascally activities we get up to.

Disclaimer:
Please do not attempt to try and copy any of the events that you read in this book, unless your little monkey becomes unruly and whispers in your ear.

Thanks, Archie 6 3/4

The Best Cake In The Whole Universe

It was the morning of the first weekend of the summer holidays. A storm had erupted overnight, leaving the ground soaking wet. Luckily the sun was shining brightly from over the hillside, and it's rays gradually dried the land.

Archie, Sophie, and Micky the Monkey were sitting in the back of the car on their way to their grandparent's after visiting the local bakery. As they travelled along the country roads, Sophie watched falling leaves turn in the wind. She giggled as she thought they spun like tiny brown and yellow ballerinas on their tiptoes. Archie could not take his mind off the cakes they had just bought, their smell was becoming overpowering. His nose twitched like a rabbit's, his mouth watered and his stomach began to rumble.

Restless, Archie turned fidgety while Micky whispered into his ear and pointed at the cake-filled paper bag. With his eyes locked on the bag, Archie wondered, *I suppose I could take just the one bite.*

He stretched out an arm, but he couldn't quite reach the bag. He needed another way of getting it. Again, Micky whispered into his ear.

'Good idea!' Archie said with a smirk, before slumping forward in his seat. He stretched out a leg and hooked his foot around the bag and pulled it towards him.

'What are you doing?' asked Sophie as she turned around.

SHHHHH! 'Be quiet!' went Archie. 'Micky said we can have a bite of our cakes if we're quiet.' He opened the bag and peered inside. Staring back at him were five delicious cakes, all saying, 'Eat me!'

Archie swallowed hard.

The smell drifting out was amazing – he could almost taste them. Licking his lips, he reached inside, pulled one out, and raised it to his wide-open mouth and bit down. It was delicious – it tasted like the best cake in the whole universe.

Suddenly his father shouted from the front seat, 'Archie! What are you doing?!'

'Huh!' Archie gasped and dropped the cake. 'Erm, nothing!' he quickly replied, wiping his mouth.

His father was not convinced. 'I hope you're not trying to take a sneaky bite of the cakes?'

'I wasn't!' Archie promised before licking his lips.

'Hmm. OK, as long as you're not. It would be nice to eat them together,' added his father, still unconvinced.

They shortly arrived, and as soon as they pulled onto the driveway, Archie unfastened his seat belt, grabbed the bag and jumped out of the car.

'I've got the cakes already, Dad!' he called out over his shoulder as he quickly ran across the driveway. He burst through the front door, yelling, 'We've got cakes!' before kicking off his trainers and leaving them in a pile at the bottom of the stairs.

'Have you? Good boy!' Grandad responded, rubbing his hands together as he sat in his armchair in the lounge. 'See your grandma – she's in the kitchen.'

Archie took the cakes with him into the kitchen, where he found Grandma with a white teapot in her hand and steam billowing out of the kettle's spout.

'Hello, Archie,' she said as he entered.

'We've got cakes, Grandma,' said Archie, placing the bag on the worktop.

'Good timing, I've just put the kettle on,' she said before opening a cupboard. Grandma pulled out some small plates, and Archie watched her pluck the cakes one by one from the bag. 'Huh!' he suddenly gasped. Archie realised, any second now, Grandma was going to discover one of the cakes had a bite out of it!

'Oh, what's this?' Grandma said, pulling out the final cake. 'It looks like a mouse has nibbled through the bag and helped itself!' She peered down over her glasses at Archie.

'It wasn't my idea, Micky told me to do it!'

Grandma frowned and shook her head. 'What would you and your sister like to drink?' She asked as she poured steaming hot water from the kettle into the teapot.

'Lemonade, please,' Archie replied.

Grandma walked to the other side of the kitchen, slid open a tall, narrow drawer, and pulled out a large bottle of clear, bubbly liquid.

PIFIZZZZZZ! went the bubbles as she twisted the cap.

'Here you go,' she said, handing Archie a glass filled with lemonade.

'Thank you,' Archie said as he held his drink. He took a huge sip, but it was far too fizzy; the bubbles instantly began to pop in his mouth - filling his eyes with tears. The exploding fizz was too much – Archie thought his mouth was going to burst! He swallowed hard. All of a sudden:

BBBBBUUUUURRRRPPPPP!

'Archie!' cried Grandma.

'Pardon me,' Archie said sheepishly, before giggling.

'Come on,' Grandma said, picking up a tea tray. 'Let's join the others.'

Archie followed her into the lounge and sat on the big crimson rug where he began to rip off the white, sugary topping from his cake and dropped it into his mouth. Eating the cake felt glorious, he wished it went go on forever and ever and ever - like it was the most enormous cake in the whole, wide world. Sadly it was just a normal size cake and the feeling quickly faded– leaving him restless. Micky whispered into Archie's ear. Archie thought about Micky's idea for a second, then asked Grandad if he could feed the fish in the garden pond.

'Of course you can,' Grandad replied. 'You will find the fish food in the shed.'

The Secret Through The Ivy

With a long, slow pull on the handle, Archie gradually opened the door to Grandad's crooked, old, shed. The shed smelt of damp wood and petrol from the lawnmower and the door creaked as Sophie peered through the gap. It was dark inside, but she could still spot giant cobwebs hanging from the ceiling, gardening tools leaning against the walls and a pair of old, wrinkly boots covered with mud. As they crept inside across the squeaky floorboards, Archie and Sophie searched the dusty shelves stacked with tins of rusty nuts n bolts, paint pots and random odd gloves for the tub of fish food.

'Found it!' cheered Archie as he discovered the pot high up. He stood on tiptoes to lift it down.

With fish food now in hand, they made their way through the Ivy arch to the pond. Brightly coloured flowers filled with buzzing bumblebees lined the path, and blackbirds tweeted from the trees above. Sophie hopped, skipped and jumped cracks in the paving while Archie shook the pot of fish food like maracas. When they reached the pond, Archie knelt and tossed some food into the water. Ripples drifted out then cleared, allowing him and Sophie to see the fish feeding. One by one they appeared from the dark depths with their mouths open wide, ready to suck up the pellets like a hoover. Archie smiled as the golden fish took it in turns to gulp their food. Suddenly a frog leapt from a rock and splashed into the water.

'Cool!' Archie cried, applauding the frog's dynamic dive. A turquoise dragonfly began to hover above, rapidly flapping its delicate wings. It darted from side to side before landing on top of a reed. Sophie smiled, admiring its bright green and blue colours, just as a water boatman gently skimmed across the pond.

Archie giggled and said, 'You look like you're in a boat!'

As he watched it glide across, its tiny oar-like legs formed little waves. Micky whispered into Archie's ear. Archie thought about what Micky had said, then looked along the ground and found a stone. He picked it up and threw it into the pond.

PLOP!

The fish scattered beneath the weeds and the frog hid under a lily pad. Amused, Archie giggled and picked up another stone and threw it into the pond. The fish poked their noses out but quickly backed away as it whizzed past.

'Why are you doing that?' asked Sophie.

'Micky said to do it, and I like the sound the stones make as they hit the water!' Archie replied. Micky sat on the pond's edge and tugged on Archie's shorts just as he raised his hand to throw another stone. Archie bent down, and Micky whispered something else into his ear. Archie hesitated before bending down and picking up lots more stones.

Armed with a handful, he stretched his arm back and with a big lob launched his ammunition.

PLOP! PLOP! PLOP! PLOP! PLOP!

The fish and frog shuddered as the stones zoomed past them like torpedoes.

'That sounded awesome!' Archie said, gloating.

'They sounded like a drum!' added Sophie.

Micky wiped his tuft of hair free from pond water and pointed to a large rock.

Archie scratched his chin and said, 'I wonder what sort of sound *that* would make?' and walked around the pond to investigate. Squatting down behind the big grey boulder, Archie cupped his hands underneath it. His face glowed red, and he made a grunting sound as he pulled and tugged on the stone. He huffed and puffed and tensed every muscle in his body, but it was no good – the rock would *not* budge.

'What are you doing now?' asked Sophie, frowning at her flustered brother.

Exhausted, Archie stood back up and replied, 'I bet this big rock will sound like a louder drum as it hits the water, but it's too heavy for me to lift.' He looked down and noticed Micky was making a pushing motion with his hands.

'Of course!' Archie realised. 'The rock is too big for me to lift, but we can push it! Come on, Lil Sophie, help me.'
With Sophie's help, the rock broke free and rolled towards the pond.

SPLASH!

The rock hit the water with so much force it snapped the dragonfly's reed. Frightened, it flew away. So shocked were the fish, they gulped before diving for cover. The frog croaked loudly and leapt out of the pond with a huge jump. The water boatman burst over the pond's edge with the tidal-like wave caused by the rock's impact.

'Yay! We did it!' Archie cheered as he watched waves lap over the side of the pond.

'But where have all the fish gone?' Sophie asked as the water eventually settled.

Archie looked into the pond, all he could see were their reflections staring back at him. 'Where's the frog?, the dragonfly *and* the little bug that looks like he's in a boat?!' he curiously wondered.

A light breeze swept through the garden - gently rustling the bamboo leaves.

'Hello, Sophie,' said a gentle voice.

Sophie turned to her brother and frowned. 'Why did you say my name in a silly voice?' she said.

'It wasn't me!' Archie promised.

'Hmm.' Sophie was unconvinced.

Suddenly the voice returned, 'hello, Sophie.'

'Huh!' Sophie gasped and quickly turned, but there was no one there.

'Hello, Archie.' The mysterious voice *now* began to greet Archie.

Archie turned and began to search the garden. He looked left, then right, under the table and chairs and behind the big oak tree, but he couldn't find a single person! He began to giggle. *Maybe it's Grandad playing games?* he thought, and called for him, 'Grandad!' nothing. Grandad, didn't reply. All Archie could hear were the blackbirds singing high in the trees and a dog in the far distance barking. He was confused. 'I'll find out who you are!' he called out.

The mysterious voice returned, 'Hello, Sophie and Archie,'

'Huh!' Sophie gasped and looked at Archie in shock.

Archie frowned and said, 'Right! That's it! I'm going to find out who you are once and for all!' he swiftly turned to catch their surprise visitor.

Then he searched left, right, under the tables and chairs, behind the big oak tree and even inside the crooked, old, shed but still he could not find anyone! *It's got to be Grandad*, he thought. He giggled again and said, 'Grandad, I know it's you. Come out, come out, wherever you are!' he stood motionless, awaiting Grandad's reply, but again, nothing. All Archie could hear were the blackbirds singing high in the trees, and the dog in the far distance was still barking! Placing his hands on his hips, Archie stomped a foot on the ground. 'This isn't funny any more!' he yelled before returning to the pond in a sulk.

Then the voice made *another* return, 'You can be quite mischievous at times,' it said.

Archie rolled his eyes and shook his head in disappointment. 'I know it's you, Grandad, you can stop it now, it's not funny any more.'

'It is not your grandad – it is I,' the voice replied.

'Huh!' Sophie gasped, then said nervously, 'It sounded like it was coming from over there...' she looked up towards an ancient stone statue, a bald-headed old man dressed in robes and sandals. The carved figure sat cross-legged on a rock, beside the bamboo. One hand rested on top of his twisted staff while the other slowly stroked his long, wispy beard.

The statue chuckled, then said, 'Yes, it has been me all along.'

Sophie giggled before asking nervously, 'What's your name?'

'My name is Yontan,' replied the statue. 'Pushing the big rock into the pond was destructive,' he began. 'I have seen you both in the past, admiring the fish as they glide amongst the weeds.'

'They are amazing swimmers!' Archie confirmed.

'Do you see them swim now?' asked the stone figure.

Archie peered into the pond. 'No,' he replied, looking back up.

'Did you enjoy the frog leaping today, Sophie?' asked the statue.

'Yes, I did, he is a good jumper!'

'Is the frog leaping now?'

Sophie looked towards the frog's empty lily pad and replied, 'no, he's not.'

'The dragonfly took a rest upon the reed – where is that dragonfly now?'

Archie looked at the reed crumpled under the rock. 'Oh...' he said, saddened.

'Can you see anything of the water boatman Sophie?' Yontan asked.

Sophie searched for the tiny bug but couldn't see it. She pouted her bottom lip, sank her head and said sadly, 'It's not there, I can't see it.'

'All the wonderful creatures you have been admiring today live in the pond,' said Yontan. 'When the rock rolled and splashed into it, they fled and sought refuge wherever they could. The frog croaked loudly and hopped out. The fish dived deeply, the dragonfly flew away, and the water that splashed over the edge carried out the water boatman.'

Upset, Archie said, 'I'm sorry, I didn't realise. Micky said I should do it.'

'Listen,' Yontan insisted, pointing to the sky. 'Tell me, what can you hear?'

Silently, Archie stood still as he listened.

'Well?' asked the statue.

'I can't hear anything,' Archie eventually replied.

'Nothing at all?'

Remaining silent, Archie listened again. Still, he could not hear anything. No blackbirds singing high in the trees, no bees buzzing and even the dog in the far distance had stopped barking.

It felt like every bird and animal close by had disappeared!

'I can't hear anything,' Archie repeated.

A cloud drifted in front of the sun. The temperature dropped, sending a shiver down Archie's spine.

'They are all connected,' said Yontan. 'The vibrations of the rock splashing into the pond echoed far and wide, upsetting all the living creatures.'

Upset, Archie dropped his head and sniffed as a tear formed in the corner of his eye.

'Do not be upset, Archie,' reassured the statue. 'Would you like to see the agile fish swim amongst the weeds again? To see the frog leap?'

Archie wiped his nose with the back of his hand and nodded.

'Sophie would you like to see the dragonfly with its crazy colours fly again, and the water boatman glide across the pond?'

'Yes, please,' she replied.

'To hear the bumblebees buzz, the blackbirds sing and the dog bark?'

Archie wiped the tear rolling down his cheek and sobbed, 'But how? We've upset them – now they are gone.'

'I shall tell you a secret - but first, you must not pay attention to Micky,' Yontan advised.

Archie frowned and scratched his head – he was confused.

'Micky will get you into trouble,' Yontan warned. 'The secret is to focus your attention on something calming - like the stillness of the pond's water,' he added. 'Then, take a deep breath, smile, and feel happy. You will start to glow, and it will change the whole world around you. All the creatures in the land will see you smile, feel your happiness and return, bringing you joy. You can join in too Sophie, look I'll show you how.'

Sophie watched Yontan rest both hands on his twisted stick and breathe in a big breath through his nose and let it out through his mouth.

Gazing back into the pond, Sophie and Archie hesitantly began to copy Yontan.

'Good,' Yontan applauded, admiring their efforts. 'Now, as you stay smiling Archie, does Micky whisper into your ear?'

Archie waited for Micky's whisper and replied, 'No, he doesn't.'

'Very good – now smile bigger. The bigger, the better, the bigger the smile, the brighter your teeth will shine. The bigger the smile, the more you will glow, and your eyes will sparkle - just like stars in the night's sky. The bigger the smile, the happier you will feel.'

Archie smiled bigger, knocking tears from the corners of his eyes. He wiped them free as they started to glide down his cheeks.

'That is *very* good!' Yontan cheered. 'Now continue to look into the clear pond and focus on the calmness and stillness of the water.'

As Archie and Sophie looked into the still pond at their smiling mirrored faces, Archie smiled a bigger smile revealing his pearly white teeth. He noticed his eyes *did* sparkle like stars in the night's sky.

A light breeze swept by, drifting the clouds away from the sun. The bamboo swayed gently, making a slight rustling sound.

RIBBIT!

'The frog!' Sophie gasped. She looked up to find the frog sitting on top of a lily pad.

'Cool!' Archie cheered as its big, black, shiny, googly eyes blinked at him.

'Tell me, what do you now see?' Yontan asked patiently. Sunlight bounced off a fish's golden scales while it zigzagged amongst the weeds.

'A fish! I've just seen a fish! Look Archie there's a fish!' Sophie cheered happily pointing.

Gradually the creatures returned. The dragonfly hovered, the water boatman rowed, the dog barked and in the trees, a blackbird began to sing.

Grinning from ear to ear Archie and Sophie leapt up, punched the sky, and cheered, 'Yay! They're back, they're back, they're back!'

Pete's Sweets

The next morning Archie and Sophie woke early. Excited to see their new friend, they quickly dressed and ran downstairs. When they entered the kitchen and looked through the big glass door, they discovered Grandad in the garden, mowing the lawn.

Grandma came in behind them and said, 'Who are you two looking for?'

'Oh, nobody,' Archie quickly replied and winked at Sophie as she tried to hide her giggle behind her hand.

Grandma flicked the kettle on, and the children began to eat their breakfast at the table. As they ate their cereal, Archie and Sophie watched Grandad finish cutting the grass and stow the lawnmower back into the shed.

'Morning kids,' he said as he entered the house. 'Would you like to come to the shops with me? - 'We can ride there on my new scooter.'

'Yeah!' Archie and Sophie cheered and quickly jumped down from the table.

'Go and get your trainers on,' Grandad added as he shuffled along, clutching his walking stick.

Archie and his sister ran to the hallway, sat on the stairs, and pulled on their shiny, white trainers.

Grandad stood in front of the mirror and put on his flat cap. 'Are you ready?' he asked, pulling on the handle of the front door.

'Yeah!' Archie and Sophie eagerly replied as they stood up. Grandad opened the door and stepped out with them close behind. They opened the garage door together to reveal his gleaming new, red scooter.

'Awesome!' cheered Archie, admiring the polished, metallic red-and-black striped cart with its big, chunky, black tyres, leather seat, and basket on the front.

Grandad shuffled closer, hooked his walking stick over the back of the seat, and sat down. 'Jump on then kids,' he said, pulling on a pair of black fingerless gloves he retrieved from the basket.

Archie and Sophie jumped onto the scooter, and Micky leapt into the basket.

'We'd better put these on, so we don't get flies in our eyes,' Added Grandad. He handed Archie and Sophie a pair of goggles.

They took them from Grandad and pulled them down over their eyes, making them look like old fashioned racing car drivers!

'Now whatever you do, do *not* push *that* button,' Grandad insisted, pointing.

Archie and Sophie looked down. In front of them glared a big, red button from the dashboard.

'Right, are you ready?' Grandad asked as he turned the key.

'Yeah!' replied the excited children.

'Hold on tight,' Grandad advised before squeezing on a lever on the handlebars. The scooter zoomed out of the garage and up the sloped driveway. They travelled so quickly, Sophie thought they were going to jump like a stunt driver as they left the curb!

With the children between Grandad's legs, gripping the handlebars, they whizzed along the pathway. It wasn't long before Micky tapped on Archie's hand, whispered into his ear, then pointed at the red button.

'What are you doing?' asked Sophie, noticing Archie staring at the button. 'No!' she yelled as his finger hovered over it, 'Grandad said not to!'

It was too late; Archie pushed the red button. Suddenly the

scooter's front wheels reared up like a wild horse.

WOOOOOSHHHHHH!

They zoomed off like a speeding rocket to the moon. The scooter

accelerated with such a high speed, poor Sophie could barely hold

on, and Micky almost fell out of the basket!

'Woaaaahhhhh!' cried Archie as he fell into Grandad's lap.

   'Arrrrcccchhhiiiieeee! I told you *not* to push that

butttttoooooonnnn!' Grandad yelled as he desperately held on.

He frantically steered them around an old lady on a much slower scooter. Her long skirt blew up over her face - revealing her big, pink, frilly knickers! She skidded before falling into a ditch! Further along, they whizzed past a couple of dog walkers whose dogs barked and growled as their leads tangled into a knot.

As Grandad's speeding scooter charged along in a cloud of dust, the wind rushed hard into everyone's face. Sophie's long locks of hair flared out behind her like a troll's, while Archie's goggles steamed up. Grandad's cap spun on top of his head, twisting it backward, and his walking stick nearly unhooked itself from the back of the chair! Micky didn't have time to hide – the wind was so strong, it blew his lips wide open, revealing his gnashing teeth. He looked like a snarling wolf! Using all of their strength, Archie and Sophie gripped the handlebars so tightly their knuckles turned white like they were riding a roller coaster.

The thrill of the ride was exhilarating to Archie; he couldn't help but giggle. In fact - he was still chuckling as Grandad ground the scooter to a halt. With a huge skid that left black smoke and the smell of burning rubber in their wake, Grandad and the kids came to a standstill outside Pete's Sweets.

Trying to catch his breath, Grandad puffed, 'Here's… some… pocket… money.'

Archie and Sophie raised their goggles high on their heads as Grandad placed a big, gold coin that shimmered in the sun in the palm of their hands.

'Wow! Thanks, Grandad!' they said, before running into the shop - clutching the money tightly. So thrilled, they ran past the shelves of magazines and comics, straight to the sweet counter.

Standing behind the counter was Pete, a well-dressed man with a shiny bald head, big, bushy, black beard and thick, round glasses which made his eyes look far too big for his face.

Behind Pete were shelves upon shelves, upon shelves of large, glass jars filled with every type of sweet you could imagine. Fizzy cola bottles, fat-bellied jelly babies, and sherbet flying saucers sat waiting, ready to be eaten by small boys and girls, like Archie and Sophie. Spellbound by the rainbow of brightly coloured jars, Archie and Sophie stood on tiptoe to peer over the counter.

As Archie scanned the racks, he grew overwhelmed at the sheer choice and couldn't decide what he wanted. Micky whispered into his ear and pointed to some crumbly, broken shards and heaps of sugary dust laying at the bottom of an almost empty jar. Archie chewed the side of his mouth as he thought about Micky's suggestion.

'You're right,' he eventually said. 'I will get all that sugar at the bottom if I choose from that jar.' He handed over his big, shiny, gold coin and waited for his sister before re-joining Grandad.

'Are you all done?' Grandad asked, looking up from his newspaper.

Archie nodded, placed his and Sophie's sweets in the basket, and watched Micky jump back in before climbing on. Grandad folded his newspaper and put it into the pocket on the back of his chair before starting the engine.

'Whatever you do, *don't* push *that* button,' he said sternly as they set off.

'I won't,' Archie promised smirking, while he pulled down his goggles back over his eyes.

All That Has A Buzz Is Not A Wasp

'Watch out for the nasty wasps from the apple tree, they like sweet things – they may sting you,' Grandad warned as Archie led his sister through the side gate into the back garden.

Sitting on the lawn listening to the sounds of seagulls squawking from the rooftops and lawnmowers from neighbouring houses, Archie opened his bag of sweets and peered inside. He pulled out a hard lump of sticky candy and popped it into his mouth. The delicious mouth-watering sweet dissolving in his mouth and the warm sun beating down on him made a great combination. He closed his eyes and smiled. The sweet tasted so good, and the sun felt so warm – he was enjoying every second of it. He began to wiggle his hips in a merry eating jig, but it wasn't long before the sweet melted, and his happy feeling faded.

Micky disturbed him with a tap on his shoulder and a whisper in his ear. Archie opened his eyes. Micky was pointing to the sweet bag and acting like he was pouring its contents into his mouth. Archie licked his lips and thought about Micky's idea. He was unsure and hesitant, then suddenly picked up the bag and poured some of the sugary dust into his mouth.

COUGH!

Immediately Archie choked. The overpowering sweet powder made him cough - the fizzing sugar tickled the back of his throat. Archie had poured too much into his mouth! It started to spill out of his nose in a sticky snot drip.

'Eww, that's gross!' moaned Sophie as she watched her brother wipe the bubbling bogey away with the back of his hand.

The heat from the sun began to make the children feel drowsy. They laid down and looked up at the pale blue sky and watched the white, fluffy clouds gently float by.

Soon, they fell into a snooze. Archie couldn't fully relax – he was worried a wasp was coming to attack him for his sweets just as Grandad had warned. All of a sudden, he felt something crawling on his legs! In a panic, he quickly flicked his eyes open to discover a trail of ants scurrying over his shins! Each twitching ant frantically grasped a grain of sugar from his sweet bag. Archie watched the little, black creatures march over his body. One by one, they stepped like a platoon of tiny soldiers stomping through the blades of grass carrying the white sugar.

Fixated with the busy working insects, Archie woke his sister,

'Look, Sophie, let's find out where they are going.'

Archie and Sophie crawled on their hands and knees following the ants to the bottom of the garden.

As they reached the pond, Sophie asked, 'Can you see the fish?'

'No, maybe they're waiting for some food,' replied Archie. He stood up to fetch the tub of fish food, but Micky tugged on his shorts. Archie bent down, and Micky whispered into his ear.

'I could feed them, sweets,' he said as he thought about Micky's suggestion. He opened his bag of sweets, selected a few lumps, and tossed them into the pond.

'What are you doing?' Asked Sophie. 'Do you remember what Yontan said?'

'But *everyone* likes sweets!' Archie replied.

PLOP! PLOP! PLOP! PLOP!

The sweet lumps splashed down, creating ripples as they broke the water's surface. One by one, the golden fish slowly made an appearance from the murky depths. Archie smiled as he watched them rise to the surface with their mouths open, ready to suck up the sinking sugar treats. 'You see Sophie, I told you everyone likes sweets.' he said, pointing at the fish. But to Archie's surprise, they immediately spat them out. With a look of disgust, they hid amongst the weeds. Archie frowned – he was confused. Micky whispered something else into his ear. 'Hm, I don't know,' he said hesitantly. 'Maybe you're right. Maybe the lumps are too hard.' Archie shook his bag of sweets and poured sugary, dusty flakes into the water. It fizzed like a glass of freshly poured lemonade.

RIBBIT!

'Huh!' Sophie gasped as the frog croaked from a lily pad. It gulped at the falling flakes, but quickly coughed out a big fizzing bubble.

It popped on a rock - sending clouds of foam across the pond.

Amused Archie giggled. 'The frog looked like he burped a great, big ball of dust!'

The frog jumped off the lily pad and dived under a rock.

Eventually, the pond settled.

A delicate wind flowed through the garden causing the bamboo to sway and a gentle voice greeted Archie and Sophie.

'Hello, children,' it said.

'Yontan!' cheered Archie and Sophie, happy to see their new friend.

Sat beside the bamboo with his hands resting on top of his crooked staff, Yontan asked, 'Can you see the fish weave their flexible bodies through the weeds?'

Brother and sister turned back to the pond. 'No,' they replied.

'And the frog leap?'

Once again, Archie and Sophie searched over the pond, 'No,' they again replied.

'Why do you think that could be?' Yontan asked.

Archie scratched his chin as he tried to think, 'I don't know,' he eventually replied.

'Fish and frogs do not like sweets. Did you not see them spit it out, or cough? They are now upset and have hidden from view. The fish retreated to the weeds, and the frog dived under a rock.

'I'm sorry, Micky told me to do it, and I thought everyone liked sweets,' Archie replied.

'Not everyone is the same,' Yontan began. 'We are all different. We must accept that. Have you not learned anything of my teachings from the past?' He slowly stroked his long wispy beard while he waited for Archie to answer.

'Yes, I have,' Archie shamefully replied.

'Yes?' asked the statue. 'Then tell me, what must you do?'

Archie slowly responded, 'First... I must not pay attention to Micky.'

'Then why is it that you pay him so much attention?' Yontan asked as he quickly flicked his beard out of his lap with a sharp flick of his wrist.

'Because...'

'Yes, go on,'

'He is very persistent.'

'You must let Micky's probing ideas drift past you like the clouds in the pale blue sky,' Yontan pointed up. 'If you pay Micky attention, what will happen?'

'He will get me into trouble,' replied Archie sheepishly.

'What is it you must do to not pay Micky the attention he so seeks, to see the reappearance of the wonderful creatures you so admire?'

'The secret,' Archie replied. 'I need to focus my attention on something calm, like the water in the pond, then take a deep breath.'

'And then?'

'Smile and feel happy!' interrupted Sophie.

Yontan smiled at the young girl's enthusiasm as Archie continued.

'Smile, and my eyes will sparkle - just like the stars in the night's sky. The more I smile, the more I will glow, and the happier I will feel. All the creatures in the land will see my smile and feel my happiness, and return - bringing me joy.'

'Good! Well done,' Yontan applauded. 'Now, do as you say. Don't forget, Sophie; you can join in too.'

Archie and Sophie gazed into the pond and breathed in a big breath, filling their lungs with air before slowly releasing it and smiling. While they watched their smiling mirrored faces, a shoal of fish slowly swam past.

'Tell me, what do you see?' Yontan patiently asked.

'The fish!' Sophie cheered, just as the frog crawled out from under the rock and onto a lily pad.

50

'And the frog!' Archie happily cheered. 'Yay! They've come back!'

Suddenly there was a buzzing sound approaching from behind. Afraid, Sophie gasped, 'huh! The wasp!'

Feeling her nervousness, Yontan spoke calmly, 'do not be afraid. Do not let what you have been led to believe to be the truth. You are anxious and agitated about the wasp, your belief of it wanting to harm you has clouded your mind.

Now, both of you look back into the pond – look at how clear it is.'

Sophie and Archie peered back into the pond.

'Pay attention to how pure the water is and how clearly you can see,' Yontan advised. 'Focus on the calmness of the pond, the stillness of the water's surface. Stayed focused on the water and take another deep breath.'

Archie and Sophie raised their chins and breathed in deeply.

'Do you feel tranquil like the water?' Yontan asked as he slowly stroked his beard.

'Yes,' the children replied.

The hum of the buzz returned, and Yontan said, 'now you must face what is coming.'
The siblings began to turn to confront the wasp.

'Remember, you must remain calm, smile, and feel happy. Your head must be clear like the pond's water is pure.'

'A bumblebee!' Sophie cheered when she discovered the buzzing sound was a bee and not a wasp! It flew right past her and bounced over the fence.

'Well done,' Yontan congratulated. 'You both remained calm, your angst over the wasp faded, and with a clear head, you were able to focus. All that has a buzz is not a wasp.'

All of a sudden, the bamboo rustled as a breeze swept through the garden. A few light raindrops began to fall, making a soft pitter-patter sound as they hit the ground. Sophie looked up to the sky and sighed, 'Oh no, it's raining.'

'Do not be disappointed,' Yontan reassured her. 'It is merely a sun shower; you can feel the glory of its power all around you. The pond needs rain for the fish and frog to survive, and the flowers need water to bloom. Just look.' He pointed over her shoulder.

Sophie turned to witness a blue and violet butterfly. Like a snowflake caught in the wind, it fluttered past her. In awe, she marvelled at it while it landed on a pink rose and slowly opened and closed its delicate sapphire wings.

'Is it not beautiful?' Yontan asked, observing Sophie's admiration.

Watching the butterfly take off again, Sophie smiled once more and said, 'It *is* beautiful.'

Grandad's Fall

The rain fell all night and had only just stopped before Archie and Sophie woke the next morning. They went downstairs and spotted Grandad in the front garden raking up leaves from the lawn, 'Morning, kids,' he said as they joined him.

'Morning, Grandad,' the children replied as they stood next to his wheelbarrow. *Wow! that's a big pile of leaves!* Archie thought. The heap of leaves next to Grandad's wheelbarrow was so tall, it was taller than he was!

'I've saved some big ones, they are in my coat pocket,' Grandad instructed, pointing to his coat hanging from a tree branch. As Archie began to rummage through the coat pockets, Grandad added, 'There may be some toffees in there too if you're lucky.'

56

Archie smiled, carried on with his search, and pulled out a rusty old nail, a couple of toffees wrapped in shiny red wrappers and three giant leaves!

'Wow!' said Sophie, amazed at the size of the enormous leaves in her brother's hand.

'Thanks, Grandad!' Archie said, before unwrapping one of the toffees. Instantly his mouth watered as the brown, hard, buttery sweet began to melt on his tongue.

'I'm going into the back garden now,' Grandad said as he unhooked his jacket from the tree. 'Do you want a ride in the wheelbarrow?'

'Yeah!' cheered Archie and Sophie as they climbed into the wheelbarrow.

Grandad picked up the wheelbarrow and wheeled the children through the side gate.

A rich, earthy smell rising from the pile of old, crumbling wood next to the compost heap tickled Sophie's nose. She almost sneezed while her nose twitched.

Grandad said, 'I bet if I lift one of those logs, we will see loads of creepy crawlies. Shall we take a look?' As soon as he picked up a log from the stack, lots of tiny creatures panicked and ran. Shiny millipedes with their hundreds of legs, scaly woodlice, and small, shiny, black beetles darted in all different directions looking for somewhere to hide.

'Wow!' said Archie, amazed at the frantic activity of the insects.

Suddenly there was a strange noise coming from above.

HONK! HONK! HONK!

Everyone looked up to find a flock of grey geese honking like an old-fashioned car.

'Can we see if the fish are in the pond?' Archie asked as the birds flying in an arrow shape disappeared through the darkening clouds.

'Of course you can, but I'm not sure how many you'll be able to see – the pond is covered with leaves.' Grandad replied.

'Come on, Lil Sophie, let's take a look,' said Archie to his sister.

Nearing the pond, Archie could see Grandad was right – it was covered with leaves. He knelt, but couldn't see any fish. Micky sat on the pond's edge and tapped Archie's shoulder. Archie turned, and Micky whispered into his ear. Archie thought about Micky's idea for a while. Eventually he picked up a stone and raised his arm. Suddenly he lowered it again. Archie had remembered what Yontan had taught him. 'I'm not going to throw stones into the pond,' he said. 'It's covered with leaves. I can't see clearly – I might hit a fish or the frog, I'm not doing it.

I want to see the fish!' Archie dropped the stone and asked Sophie to help him make a clearing. Together they plucked out the soaking wet leaves and laid them on the ground. While they swept, small waves gently lapped up in front of them.

Once again, Micky tried to get Archie's attention and whisper in his ear. Archie considered Micky's new idea and began to search his pocket but, suddenly stopped. 'No, I'm not going to feed the fish toffees,' he said. 'They don't like sweets – they cough them out.' Archie continued to clear the pond. By the time he and Sophie had removed as many leaves as they could reach, the water settled to a stillness. They smiled. As Archie smiled, he caught a glimpse of his grinning reflection, then suddenly realised. 'Of course!' He said. 'The secret!'

As Archie peered at the calm water, he drew in a big breath of air through his nose and slowly released it out of his mouth and smiled. Micky didn't whisper into his ear.

Keeping his focus, Archie noticed a flash of golden scales flicker in front of him. 'Huh!' he gasped, his smile grew bigger. With his teeth flashing white and his eyes twinkling, a great, big, golden fish suddenly appeared from the murky, dark depths. It was the biggest Archie had ever seen! The fish swam faster than the rest and, like a dolphin jumping waves in the ocean - it leapt out of the water!

'Wow!' the children cheered.

A light wind swept across the garden, the bamboo rustled and a gentle voice said, 'Hello, children.'

'Yontan!' Archie and Sophie cheered and looked up.

'You did well today,' Yontan began.

'Thank you,' said Archie.

'Micky was trying to get your attention, was he not?' The statue asked as he began to slowly stroke his beard.

'Yes, he was,' agreed Archie.

'What did you do not to pay him the attention he so eagerly wanted?'

'I remembered the secret.'

Yontan returned his hand to his crooked staff and raised a small smile. 'Very good. I am impressed. Did you see anything in the pond as you smiled, Archie?' Yontan continued.

'I did,' replied Archie.

'Tell me, what did you see?'

'A massive fish!' Sophie interrupted.

'I've never seen one so big! And it jumped out of the water!' added Archie.

'That is good to hear, why do you think the fish appeared before you?' Yontan asked.

Archie thought for a second then hesitantly replied, 'It was because...'

'Yes? Go on,'

'It was because of the secret. The fish felt my calmness and noticed my smile.'

Yontan admired his young pupil's confidence and said, 'Very good.'

All of a sudden, an acorn fell from the sky and bounced on the ground between the children. They looked at one another startled. Yontan chuckled at their surprise.

Archie looked up to discover a squirrel running along a branch of the big oak tree.

'Did you not know the squirrel was in the tree?' Yontan asked.

Archie turned to Yontan and replied, 'No, I didn't realise it was there.'

'Look to the pond,' Yontan instructed. 'As you pay attention to how peaceful it is, slowly take in a deep breath.'

As Archie looked into the pond, he slowly inhaled through his nose; his chest expanded while his lungs filled with air.

'Good, now do you feel calm like the water?' Yontan asked as he rested one hand on top of the other.

'I do,' replied Archie.

'Very good. As you remain calm, you will be more alert. When you are more alert, you will be more aware of your surroundings – just like a deer in the forest. You will feel a sense of things are about to happen.'

While Archie relaxed, he listened carefully to all that Yontan had to say.

'If something does not feel right,' the wise old statue continued. 'It is because it is not.'

The more Archie concentrated on the pond's water, listening to Yontan's gentle voice; he felt a weird feeling – a sense that something was not quite right. He turned, he screamed, 'Grandad!'

Grandad had dropped his rake, clutched his chest and fell to the ground.

'Quick, Sophie, get Grandma!' Archie shouted as he stood up and ran towards Grandad.

Immediately Sophie ran to the house, yanked open the big, sliding doors, and ran inside yelling, 'Grandma!'

Archie dived to his knees at Grandad's side, 'are you OK, Grandad?' he asked.

Grandad coughed and opened an eye, 'This doesn't mean you get to keep my new scooter,' he joked before coughing again and closing his eyes.

Grandma soon came running out of the house, 'I've called an ambulance,' she said. 'They're on their way.'

Archie and Grandma stayed by Grandad's side until the ambulance arrived and paramedics carried him out on a stretcher.

'He will be OK,' one of the paramedics reassured Archie as she laid Grandad in the back of the ambulance. 'If it wasn't for you, it could have been a different story. Your awareness led you to think clearly and get your sister to alert your Grandma quickly.'

Archie and Grandma returned to the house, closely followed by the paramedics.

'Well done, kids, you've probably saved your Grandad's life.' They said. 'He will be very grateful.'

Archie and Sophie looked out of the window at Yontan sitting

beside the bamboo, and smiled.

Yontan smiled back and said, 'Remember the secret -

focus, breathe, smile, and feel happy. When you smile, the whole

world smiles with you.'

WRAP UP – THREE THINGS TO REMEMBER

Yontan's top tips.

1. Don't pay your monkey the attention he so eagerly seeks, no matter how persistent he may get.
2. Focus on something else, something calm, to help you relax – like the water in Grandad's pond or your breath when you breathe in and out.
3. Slowly inhale a deep breath, let it go slowly, feel happy and relaxed with a big smile. The more you smile the more your teeth will flash and your eyes sparkle - like the stars in the nights sky.

Look out for the next book by Adam Gibbs in 2021 –
'Ronnie's Crow'

Printed in Great Britain
by Amazon